AF429895

WOMAN GO HOME

WoMaN Go HOME

By Ruth Sawh

Illustrated by Greg Sitkowski

Woman Go Home

by

Ruth Sawh

Illustrator: Greg Sitkowski

This is a work of fiction. Any resemblance between characters and living or dead people is happenstance. All rights are reserved. Except as permitted under the U.S. Copyright Act of 1976, no part of this publication may be reproduced, distributed, or transmitted in any form or by any means, or stored in any database or retrieval system, without the prior written permission from the author for any part of the manuscript or from the illustrator for any of his illustrations; or upon the author's death, her beneficiary(ies) or upon the illustrator's death, his beneficiary(ies).

Copyright © 2020 Ruth Sawh (manuscript) and Greg Sitkowski (illustrations).

All rights reserved.

ISBN: 9798644358557

*Dedicated to all whom I love, to all who love me,
and to kind hearts everywhere*

*Special thanks to Greg and to Ian for taking a chance on me
and for making it possible for us to publish this novella.*

• • •

*Thanks also to Elite Authors and its staff for bringing my
novella to.fruition.*

Table of Contents

Chapter 1

Woman Go Home

SURPRISE, SURPRISE, SURPRISE FOR ME. I thought that, except for incompetence, company or government regulations, deciding when to retire would be personal, but no, no, no.

There's "Tom, Dick, and Harry," far and wide, and nearby too, who are in my business and who want to know why I have not yet retired at 70 years old. As a professor, I continue to score well on students' evaluations and above and beyond excellent on self evaluations. I decided that after thirty years of humility and underscoring my abilities, I had earned the right to the top scores. After all, I hadn't seen an overwhelming number of professors over 70 still working, so who are those "fives"(highest possible score for each category) being reserved for? Should they go to waste? For me, teaching for so many eons was like scaling Mount Everest and claiming rarefied air; so when the head of my department asks me how I would score myself on teaching effectiveness, organization, reliability, punctuality, research, and community service, I unabashedly assert fives. No fooling around that for me anymore.

Students with Inflated Hormones

After all, I have no problem nailing my students' attention with a few tactics that I thought up over the years. I know how to strut into a classroom full of 18-year olds, how to paint on lipstick so that they stare and wonder if I am a little unhinged, and then, I know how to dress so that they are sure that I am unhinged. Then I give my joke-of-the-day spiel which could be pulled from my quiver of anecdotes. I tell about the owner of a pet penguin taking his penguin to the movies; the gossiping woman who had the tables turned on her; the inmate at the asylum who thought he was the sane one among his crazy friends; and other jokes, designed to seize their attention—to mesmerize them—and to get them eager to hear more jokes.

When I see them slobbering, waiting with bated breath for what next will issue out of my mouth, it's like, "Bam! Gottcha!" explodes in my head. Funny disappears, and serious lesson(s) of the day are conducted. I sometimes feel like a sinner for using funny tactics, but they work, and I need to keep that game of good evaluations going for me. It's how I keep my job. It's how I get promotions—a healthier paycheck—food on the table—necessities for my family, and so even though the "pathway" to doing this is sometimes, thorny, I have to persist just like many modern-day politicians who grin, take their "blows" and move on to another incident for they too must eat; they too must provide for their families, though probably in a more elaborate fashion than a humble teacher.

Based on my students' evaluations, most think they are getting value from my classes. However, other disgruntled students, like hornets, go to the rate-your-professor website and try to stir up trouble, just because their hormones are befuddled. They warn students that I am old, shaky, and still use markers on the board. They tell them that I am not on Facebook, Instagram or Insta anything, and especially not on Blackboard, so I most assuredly fall in the category of old and technologically challenged. They signal to freshmen that wretchedly wrinkled me is not what they want to wake up to for an eight a.m. or even an eight p.m. class.

Actually, they don't need to waste time publishing the facts about my age, because to jump start every semester, I tell my students that if they don't want a 70-year old teacher, I will sign a "drop" slip so that they could scoot to younger, less wrinkled pastures faster than they could say "Rumpelstiltskin."

Some stay because of their misinterpretation of the term "user friendly," that euphemism that has been tossed around by engineers and computer experts who manufacture new technology and especially by CEO's , CFO's, UFO's and various other dimwits who labor to squeeze as much money as possible from as wide a population (even from kids' piggy banks), as possible, by baiting customers to buy some irrelevant product that they promote as being so very simple to use that even a baby could work it.

However, the malleable youth apply the term to their own platforms. "User friendly," my students believe, is attaching little icons, adding cutesy smiley faces, hearts with cupids, bouquets of flowers, and so forth to their essays and other assignments. Armored with that kind of "user friendly" equipment at hand, they believe that they could engineer a high grade no matter what their essays say. In addition, they possibly think that because I have the joke-of-the-day tactic, I am a jester and easy to be fooled. They interpret my tactics as "user friendly"--easy--and that I, like a santa claus could be asked for the grade on their wish list.

In addition, I don't know where they learned the term or if it comes naturally to them, but they create quid pro quo situations by flattering, praising, and ingenuously laying apples (Which underpaid professor wants apples when there are more glorious perks to be had? For crying out loud, some of those students' parents own yachts, mini planes, and even golf courses, can't they be more generous for something as cheap as a good grade?) on my desk.

(A good grade deserves a generous perk.)

After delivering the stingy apples they boldly ask me to give them an "A"; a few, realizing that their composition skills aren't up to par, might settle for a "B", but if they earn a "C" or worst, then woe is me. They will broadcast that I have ruined their lives. With a meager "C" on their transcripts, I have dashed their dreams of becoming the doctor or CEO or whatever lofty profession they had in mind. I will burn in a hell made seven times hotter for the immensity of my transgression. If I were truly interested in creating future world leaders, I would have been wise, and I would have known that when something is given (an apple), something must be given in return (an "A"). It is a principle of fair trade that any smart professor would recognize—an equation learned by every numskull in elementary school:

Apple given to teacher = "A" for student.

Apparently, some students would prefer to sit in classes with beauty over brain. To them, I say, check your potential professor's age and any other physical attributes—height, weight, bust, waist, hips, face, length of hair, etc.—that are vital to your learning and for preparing you for a successful career. If youth and beauty will get you attuned with the best education, then you should knock on teachers' doors and check them out before registering for my class. My aim is for all students, mine or other teachers' students, to become useful and happy citizens, so if they will learn how to do that better with youth and beauty in their faces, then they should seek out those professors. I would love small classes if more students flock to younger, less technologically challenged professors. After having taught classrooms crowded with students for many years, I would celebrate small classes with fewer, god-forgive-me, tedious essays to read.

My argument is that if I am scoring "fives" on my self evaluations, and on my students' evaluations I am scoring above average, then why are some people hurrying me up to go home?

Loud-mouth Internet

There's no privacy anymore to anyone's life, because apart from regular salacious gossip about who is sleeping with whom on campus and off, the ever present loud-mouth no-respect-for-the-aged internet now proclaims everything about everyone. The very day that I turned 70, the world knew it. It was that very day that people, especially colleagues like Punxsutawney Phils stuck their heads out of their office doors to interrogate me about when I was planning to retire.

Some seem to be losing sleep over my, "I have no clue" answer. Even some whom I previously thought of as reclusive, unabashedly ask me to nail down a date for them.

What the heck? I answer, "I don't know the date. Do you?" They slither back into their offices.

Greedy Grandma

Busybodies question whether I really need the continued income. Surely, after working for so many donkey years, I have a hefty bank account. Surely, my husband is loaded with dough. Some retired ones use some funny equivocation and say, look at themselves, they are getting pensions and they are living well; surely I will get a pension too and will also live well. I ask, are all pensions equal to others? Some think so. They seem to know that exact amount in my bank account, and they pass holy judgment on me. I am a greedy pig to continue to draw a salary when there are young people—qualified graduates, fresh in the market— eager to enter the workforce, make a living for themselves, practice their skills and pay off their school loans. Can't I leave a little something for the young 'uns? They boldly preach to me, "The love of money is the root of all evil." I should be grossly ashamed of myself.

Some take a slightly different attitude. Who do I think I am? Do I want to get richer than they? I was always poorer than they are and should keep my damned self in that down low range. Do I want to buy a better house, a summer/ winter/fall/spring home; do I want to own a better car; a more chic wardrobe? Do I want to promote myself from lower middle class to middle middle? That would be close to impossible for me, but I have pulled myself out of abject poverty more than once before, so maybe I could set a goal, and if I don't get close enough to middle middle, maybe at least I would be in upper lower middle.

I am pressed to ask whether the gossipers are in touch with reality. Are they reading or hearing about the shakiness of the economy? How it jiggles up and down? Or that the cost of living is constantly upward bound? How do I know how much money is enough to save me from becoming a beggar after I retire? Should I stop working to find out, for instance, that I cannot afford doctors' bills or medical prescriptions? Am I a Lazarus to be able to rise from my death bed to go looking for a job to pay bills?

Economists say that our grandchildren will not be able to enjoy the quality of life that we are now enjoying—all because of the enormous national debt that we, baby boomers created. I have grandchildren. I wouldn't want to see them, impish as they are to me, become panhandlers because of the debt I helped to create, so I continue to work and to save so that my precious grandchildren and possibly their children could enjoy some of what I enjoyed. I might be dead when other generations are born, but while I can, I feel compelled to save for them. Why should they suffer because of my generation's waste? I wouldn't want them to chant "greedy grandma gone to her grave" at the cemetery.

(Do I want to hear this lawlessness in my grave?)

Climbing Rungs

It is common knowledge that teachers do not receive hefty salaries. To add to that injury, English professors (I am of that breed) and faculty in some other departments, teach the supposedly less valued college courses and do not earn as much as professors teaching STEM courses, or as those in other revered departments, so I have to work for more years to save what other professors' bank accounts have accumulated. In addition, I wasn't always ranked as a professor. It took many years to climb the rungs from adjunct instructor to visiting professor, from visiting to assistant professor, from assistant to associate professor, from associate to full professor, so for all those years that I was climbing, my salary was a pittance when compared to the hoity toity professors' in the hoity toity departments.

Now that I am earning a decent lower middle class salary as a full professor, I can try to compensate for the years that I was on the brink of poverty in academia, which was not an uplifting sight. Students scrutinized my shoddy dresses, my jalopy in the parking lot, my low cost housing (thanks to the internet that provides them with my address) and swore they will not be teachers. Repeatedly, like a mantra, they wrote in their essays that they wanted the "finer things in life," so will not become teachers. I cry every time I see "finer things in life," because it reminds me of my down low situation.

I now follow the wisdom that God passed down to Joseph, in biblical times, to pass on to Pharaoh. He told Pharaoh to save during their seven years of abundance so that when the seven years of drought occurred, his government would have enough to feed his people. Lo and behold, it happened as Joseph predicted, so should I be blamed for trying to follow that wise man's advice by working a bit longer so that I could be better prepared for harder times? Who knows whether famine or pestilence will occur? Modern-day environmentalists and scientists continually voice concerns for the future of mother earth and admonish us to save resources. Should I accuse those professionals of speaking balderdash and not be desirous of saving for harder times?

When I hear or read stories of people dying because they do not have food or medicine, do not live in sanitary conditions, are not able to pay doctors' bills, have no place to live, or cannot afford basic necessities, I sympathize with them; but a soft heart cannot do anything if it does not have money, so if I work past 70, I can better equip myself to help the needy. Relatives, friends, and students sometimes tell me of their hardships; what good would I be if I cannot help them?

Monkey See, Monkey Do

Some of the smartest and richest people are working past 70 years old. Supreme court justices, politicians, CEOs, CFO's, entrepreneurs, scientists, doctors, lawyers, and others continue to work, even though their acquisitions appear to be sufficient to usher them into luxurious retirement; so besides money, those intelligent people might have other reasons for working beyond 70. Maybe they believe that Charles Darwin had a slip of the tongue and intended to theorize "Survival of the Richest," maybe it's insecurity, maybe it's fear of the unknown, maybe it's their idea of keeping the blood pumping in their hearts and brains; but whatever their reasons for continuing to work, I figure that if those wealthy, intelligent people are working well into their eighties and sometimes beyond, then inductively, I should too, and so I adopted the theory, "Monkey see, monkey do."We teach our children and students to emulate successful people, shouldn't I do so too?

(Was this what Darwin meant?)

IQs

Some of my retired challengers are asking, is my IQ superior to theirs why I continue to work after they retired at 65? Am I trying to place myself in a higher IQ bracket than theirs? Do I think I am in that category of exceptional women who become medical doctors, scientists, inventors, CEOs, lawyers, supreme court justices? How can I parallel myself with the high IQ class and continue to work?

I am not a genius for certain; I figure if I were one, I would have owned mansions, islands, airplanes, or would have had a more lucrative career, at least as a professional crook, but I certainly would have been in the uppermost class, instead of stuck in the lower middle middle. It is true that genius is not equivalent to money or reserved for the rich, but the odds seem to be against even the poor whose IQs are above average. However, in the 70 years that I have been on this earth, I continue to learn a lot, so maybe I should reassess my IQ. What if 70 is the magic number when my IQ hits genius? If so, should I put a muzzle on my new ranking?

After turning 70, I am learning more (even if it is in microscopic increments). Should I quit sharing what I am learning? What if I am on the cusp of motivating my students to concoct the elixir for eternal life? Maybe they will be able to wipe out diseases, pain, physical and mental disabilities, natural disasters, poverty, deformities, and a host of other anomalies—if only I linger a little longer.

Look at the Nobel prize winners. Are they young people? A few are, but many of them are older than 70. What if, like some of them, I am on the verge of creating logical grammar? Unearthing vocabulary of the Adam-and-Eve era? Adding nouns and verbs to our deficient language? Constructing a new form of pig latin? If my brain speaks to me and says that it wants to continue working, am I to say to it, it's time to shut your damned self down? How can I communicate with a brain that has no concept of what it means to shut down?

Liberation

I have also become liberated in a number of ways that might be beneficial to my students. For instance, when I was younger, I was not inclined to discuss sex and other sensitive topics, but now that I am older, shyness has vanished—completely. I have also liberated myself from textbooks. I used to be straight-laced and stuck to the text book—sometimes burying my head in reading long, boring passages to my suffering students, but now I *am* the textbook.

After I studied piles of texts, I know what many educators say about the subject I'm teaching, so I can look into my students' eyes, read their expressions to see if they are puzzled, and if they are, I can clarify the point I am trying to convey. Constraints to be weird, whimsical, and comical fell when I became older, and I adopted techniques (some students think "funny"), which I found to be my most valuable assets for capturing my students' attention.

Why Ask Me?

I also wonder whether any of my invigilators are asking high ranking people who are over 70, whether they plan to quit. Even our good president of "Make America Great Again" fame is over 70. Are those questioning me asking him if, or when he plans to quit? They should just try asking him. I guarantee that as the sun rises in the East and as it sinks in the West, they will receive a tweet of their lives that might teach them to keep themselves out of other people's business. That just might shut them up, and I would thank him profusely with my own tweet of adulation. We can become buddies on this issue, and maybe, just maybe, if I am lucky I might be invited to a round of golf at Mar-a-Largo, and then if I play my game right, I might even dine in style at the White House.

Party

It might be that my retired detractors want to party, to bring themselves out of their lonely little cocoons, to eat, to drink, to dance, to be merry, to be sociable; so, they suggest I have a retirement party, even though I haven't said that I am retiring—not just yet. They plan which ensemble they will wear, and out pops their pieces of fake jewelry, which they place against their cotton-laced outfits, hoping that one outfit will sparkle over the other and obliterate wrinkles from their faces. Then they go to their musty closets looking for shoes and handbag. Invariably, they will not find the perfect shoes or handbag because they never intended to find them. New shoes and new handbag mean a major outing to the mall, just what they want to draw them out of their desolate abodes.

In no way am I trying to distance myself from my friends, because I too love a party, a get-down rollicking one. I too am looking for ensembles that enhance my distressed self. I too would like to regain youthfulness, obliterate wrinkles, but a retirement party must wait and when I do have one, it will be a quiet little slink-away affair. I have seen professors go out in glory—with gala parties and glowing accolades—speeches by colleagues stating how excellent the retiree was, the same one whose job they envied and whom they prayed would evaporate, and how much that colleague will be missed, only for that very same demigod to return to humbly beg for a few hours of work. Maybe for even just one class. Returning like a dog with its tail between its legs is not a pleasing picture to me. I do not want to be like that dog.

A Tombstone

Some have found that upon retirement, the savings they once thought of as inexhaustible disappears quickly. Some miss the challenge the job once gave them. Some even miss the prettying-up—the make-up, the hair-do, the outfit, the facials, the manicures, the pedicures, the implants, the enhancements, and other such obsessions they enjoyed while working. Yet others do not know how to deal with the extra time they inherit or with the depression that engulfs them. Worst yet, some die as soon as they retire. Even thinking of the ramifications of retiring have led to massive heart attacks—in colleagues' offices—on campus. There is no doubt that retirement is a milestone to a tombstone, and some cannot deal with that. I know that I am not good at dealing with tombstone issues, so I am postponing that move for just a wee bit longer.

Travel by Wheelchair?

Another thing my friends say is, "Now is the time to enjoy life. Go travel." I have already traveled quite a bit—to over 40 different countries and islands. If I were waiting to travel after retirement, I would not have been able to fly the 24-hour trip to India without circulation problems, trudge through the remote Melakan village in Malaysia, hike up the Maracas hills to a Trinidad waterfall, climb over a hundred stairs to a tower in the El Yunque tropical forest in Puerto Rico, and more stairs to view the largest reclining Buddha in Thailand, bear the weight of a forty-pound Barbary ape that jumped on my head at the top of the Rock of Gibraltar, trek up a hill to view the active Vulcan Arenal in Costa Rica, clamber over a rocky road to an Inca village in Mexico, saunter up the grassy highlands to the Stonehenge in Great Britain, walk up Grecian hills to the ruins of the Acropolis, promenade along the Santorini heights, swim in the chilly Atlantic Ocean off Costa del sol in Spain; nor do I still have the stamina for an all-night limbo party on a cruise in the Caribbean; neither can I enjoy spicy Indian curries, or Spanish enchiladas, packed with jalapenos; my now deteriorating stomach can no longer hold a peppered mofongo from Puerto Rico; my diabetes prone self will not wolf down a whole eclair from France; I can no longer stand in the sweltering heat of a Panama zoo, and a number of other tourist activities are now beyond me.

Gratefully, I have already traveled to all of those places and several others, and have done all of those things while I was able to do them; so now, I suppose when my friends suggest future travel, they probably mean by wheel chair, because I cannot walk as far, or clamber up as many stairs as I once did. Imagine me going to Peru and not being able to climb to Machu Picchu, or to Venezuela and not able to take a bucket ride over the dizzying cliff of the Angel Falls? Do I now want to go to Switzerland and not adventure into the Alps; do I want to visit faraway countries and sit, sit, sit on the sidelines? That is not my idea of travel, so to try to lure me into renting a wheelchair and learning to manipulate it, will not work.

Volunteering

"Look at what we are doing," my retired friends say, "cooking for the homeless, tutoring kids, visiting the sick, taking meals to shut-ins." They dangle these exciting opportunities in front of me, like cheese in front of the fabled fox, but they forget that as a professor, I already have volunteering woven into my job.

I frequently volunteer to work extra hours with students. Apart from offering out-of-class tutoring, I have fed some, bought or given textbooks, offered free advice, and handed out writing utensils, etc., all with the idea of volunteering. On my supervisor's evaluations, I am not given credit for the extracurricular work I do with students. For credit from the administration, I have to publicly place myself in the presence of some big-name organization, rub shoulders a teeny weeny with the big-name organizers and get my pic in the big-name newspapers with the bosses, but that's okay with me if administration's definition of volunteering is limited, because I give myself credit for what I do in private for my students. A quiet "thank you" from a student nails it for me.

Academic Nincompoops

Besides acquaintances who are pushing for my retirement, another source of frustration comes from administrators, deans, chairpersons, and other faculty. Who would have thought that the very foundation of higher education would breed contempt? Yes, administrators and others pit young against old, like old men instigating cock fights. Some older ones, half-witted as ever for not recognizing that they too are on the brink of old age, go behind their lecterns and in glorified orations proclaim that the university needs young "blood" to be future world leaders. When young administrators and young faculty hear these proclamations, their ears perk up, their eyes dilate, and they lick their chaps with empowerment (a kind of sex drive), that is being offered them on golden platters. They place themselves on pedestals and feel as though they should indeed have the older professors' jobs. Older professors cringe and melt into their seats, hoping that no one is spying on them.

New technology has prompted this snobbery to some extent, but older administrators and heads of departments should realize that to sound like sycophants is to sink themselves into deep jeopardy of losing their positions. At that stage, when younger professors' hormones are raging more viciously than middle school bullies, administrators shouldn't risk the chance of exposing their vulnerability; instead, they could discreetly employ the necessary experts and avoid stepping up to their microphones and announcing how very, very, very badly they are bleeeeding for young people with technological know-it-all.

Truth is, not all of the younger ones know everything about technology because by the time they get out of their computer classes, etc. new techniques would have been developed. Also, many of my students know how to access Facebook, Snapchat, YouTube and other social media, but when I ask them to use proper research procedures, some do not know how to search for correct form or reliable sources on their smart phones. Those are the very students who weasel their way into the workforce in quick time.

Academic Antagonists

Another problem in academia is that some younger teachers want to teach specific courses, so if a faculty member close to retirement is teaching the course they are envious of teaching, they try to outshine the older person. They begin to publish one-line poems in abundance, so that they could accumulate more publications than the professor who is teaching the course. Then, at year-end evaluations with their bosses, they take a long list of publications as proof that they are more capable of teaching the envied course. Younger ones must be taught to have respect for older professors, and if university professors do not know that yet, then they need to be taught. So, for me, I have to keep my position to maintain some equilibrium between young and old, and pray that some of my young colleagues will learn manners.

It might sound conflicting when we think that the humanity universities are teaching is not always practiced. Some younger faculty don't care about discriminating against the old. They just want to bulldoze them and grab their courses. Words such as, "dinosaur, relic, antique, ancient, prehistoric, used-up, tired-looking," in reference to older faculty have pierced my ear drums and my heart. It is difficult to believe that such a roguish dog-eat-dog attitude has crept into academia. Do politicians know what they are talking about when they say guns should be permitted on campuses? Some young professors' and students' hormones rage more viciously than middle school bullies. Have the politicians done the math:

$$\text{Academic bullies} + \text{guns} = \text{deaths}$$

Inevitably, younger professors will become qualified for promotions and tenures, but it is only fair that they learn patience and work like older ones did.

Caveat

Despite my chagrin over nosy people constantly querying me about when I am going to retire, I am looking for signs that will tell me when it's time to say good-bye, time to pack up my little office gimcracks, time to declare instructional materials a free-for-all to colleagues, time to put a box of musty outdated books outside my door for students or passersby to spit upon, time to return my office key, time to enjoy my last merry-go-round on my shaky office chair, time to play my final game of office basketball, time to thank my boss, administrative assistant, colleagues, and other university personnel for tolerating the sight of the tottering me for so long. And then maybe, maybe if I'm not extremely peeved, I'll throw a monstrous party and say let bygones be bygones to the gossipers, even though the internet has become the number one big mouth for proclaiming my age. I am diligently searching for the signs that will lead me to that grand finale.

Before I proffer my meticulously worded letter to my boss, however, I am looking for ways to improve myself so that I do not have to make a beeline to the grave yard. I am also studying personal trends in my circumstances that might point to what I might face when the time comes for me to go home.

*(I do not want to grade one more
essay in my lifetime.)*

Chapter 2

Physical

WHEN I WAS YOUNGER, EVEN as young as in my fifties, I thought that certainly I would have retired by 60 and surely it would have been, "been there done that" by 66, which is the suggested retirement age for my age group. However, the Social Security Administration pushed retirement age to 67 for suggested reasonable benefits for those born thirteen years later than me. So I thought, why can't I do that for myself too? Since retirement age is a moving target, I would move my target too. We also know that longevity for today's population was increased; so by extension, working days have been added to everyone's lives. Hurrah, for all of us; we have more years to do what we want to do, so if I want to work, so be it.

However, I became a tad bit flustered over the multitude of questions directed towards me beginning with "When". As soon as anyone speaking to me drops, "When," out of their mouth, I vanish around a corner, but truth is, I began to question myself: what are they seeing that I cannot see? What are they hearing? Was my back seriously traveling southward? Was I not using enough makeup so that too many wrinkles were still showing? Was I walking slothfully—maybe like an inch worm, was I not shouldering my own bag of books competently, was I speaking gibberish, was I returning my students' essays with illogical comments, was I dressing like I descended from the Stone Age? What was it? Those and other skepticisms led me to work harder on both my outward appearance and my inward self.

Exercise

Health gurus and novices pontificate that exercise is necessary for maintaining a youthful figure; so, of course, I, wanting to look younger than 70, will follow their advice. I will pick myself up, park that self at the gym daily, and camp there for two hours or more, depending on my expiration date.

Prior to 70 and my liberation, I would have been too shy, too insecure, too timorous to press my chunky, rippling self into skimpy gym outfit; now, I no longer care if anyone sees me gussied up for the gym. It is the fashionable thing to do, and I have to maintain myself as a working, exercising diva. Somehow, that shame that once loomed over me like a halo when I was younger, transformed itself into a take-it-in-your-face boldness. People could he-he or haw-haw at the obvious flab showing through my outfit, but I rack that up to their insecurities. If their mama or grandmama is without a millimeter of flab, then let them laugh.

I focus on maintaining oiled joints, so that I could strut around campus with as erect a torso as any young lady. I lift weights so that I could sling my big bag of books and not look so oppressed that a student would be moved to ask if I needed help. I constantly try to melt off fat, so I pump iron and walk on the treadmill. I wish very much to be a model of good health for my students, for the naysayers, and mostly for myself. However, repeatedly, I find that, after all of the hard work, the needle on the scale does not move the slightest bit to the north; in fact, the doltish needle took the liberty to move to the south—far down. Did it ever get kicked! When I was up to 55 years old, I could lose a few pounds in a week of skipping breakfasts, but at 70, even on a largely fruit and vegetable diet (yuk!), it looks like this ambition is another of my elusive dreams.

Hair

Some older people might be blessed with heads loaded with hair, or through some other means have been able to grow artificial turf on their heads, but not all are so fortunate. I am one of the unlucky because my hair has become gray, brittle, and thin. Also, some women's ages show through their hair styles that date back to prehistoric times, but not mine. I buy trendy fashion magazines, study the latest hair-do's—the ones that the most popular young models, actresses and famously rich are wearing—then I fudge them. If they wear teased bouffants, I will tease my hair into a bouffant; if they part their hair on the side, middle, back, or wherever, I will do so too; if they wear weaves, pigtails, extensions, barrettes, bows; whatever their styles, I will duplicate them. At times the up-dos might be a mite uncomfortable, and difficult to achieve, but I remind myself of my goal—to look youthful and beautiful—so I tolerate the discomfort for the while, but that torture is too unforgiving at times that as soon as I get home, I release—usually in a raucous scream and a rush to pull down the fancy up-do. However, for me, the hair style bears silent but evident testimony that I am as young and as capable of whipping up any fashion that younger professors can erect upon their heads. Above all others, the Mohawk is my supreme choice for a never-fail bold and youthful look.

Dropped hairs leave gaping gaps on my head that are as deep as the gorges of the grand canyon, but thank God, I have techniques. I comb thicker parts over thinning parts, which I thought I invented as "parasol style," but nowadays I hear that same technique commonly referred to as a "comb over." I add extensions, and I tease the thin to look thick. I do not add extensions overnight because, due to a pinch of reasoning, my hair cannot grow long overnight. Such freakishness might obliterate my teaching success; instead of getting my students' attention, they may be shocked into a stupor, so I wait until summer break. In that way I could claim that my hair grew over several weeks. In any case, if anyone should ask whether my natural hair had truly grown to such lengths, I will send him or her a tweet of his or her life. It's the latest, proven effective method for thoroughly insulting people.

As with the tweety insults these days, the insult should make the insulted feel small, insignificant—like he or she would like to crawl into a hole in the ground, never to raise his or her blokish head again; however, some people receive tweets from high ranking officials and still roam the earth as though nothing ever happened, even when the world already knows about the gigantic insult tweeted to them that morning. That's how the insulted "save face," so I will take cue from them—take my insults and lift up my head—higher. For some people, it is the only thing to do to keep a hefty paycheck coming their way. I need a paycheck, hefty or not.

In addition, like graying others, I dye my hair, and my scalp. If some inquisitive creep creeps up behind me to search for canyon-like spaces, he or she will not be able to distinguish between scalp or hair because both hair and scalp will be of the same color. I have also furtively, under proper disguise, patronized beauty stores for wigs—several—styled after every popular young actress' hairdos. I buy my wigs in a variety of colors, and since youth tend to display their brazenness in blazing hues, I also favor reds, oranges, purples, blues, greens, silver, and gold that will brand me as a young, forward thinker. I have seen celebrities, of both sexes, boldly wearing wigs that appear to be prefabricated abodes for animals. No wonder that birds have pecked away some of those wigs in public in front of audiences, just like a barbary ape escaped with a woman's wig at the top of the rock of Gibraltar. In my case, I will wear a wig, but I will stay clear of birds, apes, babies, and clawing construction equipment.

If I goof with the hairdos, I will speed to a store to buy a nice broad-rimmed hat, and then I will cover up the fiasco and leave it there. No more worries.

If any student or students banding together as they sometimes do, wishes to investigate what's under my hat, he or she might become so traumatized by the mess under there that they will broadcast it to the student body, and no one will ever try that again. Would I care? Not a jot, not a tittle, not as long as I still have my job and I'm collecting that paycheck.

Clothes

Older people know that fashion works like a kaleidoscope—the designs change—one fashion is here today, and tomorrow there's another; so to show that I am abreast of what's trending, I inform myself of the changes. For me to keep current, is a no-brainer. As with hairstyles, I buy glossies with pictures of models and actresses, the famous and glamorous, and then I try to duplicate what they wear, in a cheaper way, of course. I search thrift stores for outfits and shoes that are similar to the ones the models wear. Often times, it's difficult to find outfits that duplicate the eccentricities that some sophisticates wear, but luckily, I took a few sewing classes in high school that help me to "cut and paste,""nip and tuck" various parts from different outfits to others so that I could contrive fashion that resemble those of the stars. Just like famous people, I wear and titivate whatever I can piece together, accessories and all, matching or clashing—with aplomb. I practice somewhat and refine the model's swagger, runway or not, on campus.

Practice in my high heeled shoes on campus, however, is sometimes limited to the classroom, since my students are my most important judges, the ones providing the end-of-term evaluations; and since oftentimes the heels are rigorously uncomfortable. Just before I perform the dramatic entrance, I discreetly pull out my high heeled shoes from my fashionable shoulder bag, slip them on, balance myself, and stage my grand entrance. Based on the finesse of my entries, I wouldn't be surprised if lurking recruiters from Milan, Italy, fashion capital of the world, will ask me to join their company.

I also take fashion cues from my female students—the ones who get the most eyes turned their way when they walk through the door. After all, my students have to stare at me for long periods, so whoever those students are looking at, I will follow, so that in turn, all students will focus on me and what I am trying to teach. Some of the ladies often wear hold-your-breath jeans, dig-into-the-bosom blouses, standing-on-a-ladder heels, and show-off-their-style hair-dos.

I do not fancy all of their styles on me, but since my goal is to get their initial attention and then to hold it for the entire period, it is logical that I will follow what's grabbing their attention. It is the smart thing to do.

Face

If botox injections, face lifts, or other methods for rejuvenating faces work, I wouldn't know; but I suspect that those methods do work, at least to some extent for some people, because those who get them hurry repeatedly to dole out large sums of money at dermatologists', cosmetologists', and voodoo practitioners' altars. Some are throwing away good money, because with each treatment they get a mite uglier, but they probably can't see the ill effects because they do not own mirrors to the 15th power as I do. I see my million wrinkles, but I will be stuck with them because the most I can afford on a teacher's salary are pleading prayers with God. If I try the face lifts, the tummy tucks, the butt boosts, the breast implants, etc., what will my family and I eat; let alone, what would I retire on?

However, it is glaringly obvious that the youthful face that God crafted for me in his wonderful image and that worked minimally for many years has now undergone tremendous evolution. Not fair, I cry to God every morning, noon and night. How could you give me something and then

grab it back? But my pleas do not diminish the lines, the fur-
rows, the chasms that appear on my forehead, mouth, and
at other strategic junctions. Those wrinkles are repeated
in magnified measure on my sagging neck so that I could
be mistaken for gobble, gobble—the one with the wattle
under his neck. I just count such ugliness as a fact of life,
so I stretch my neck as much as I can, and move on. It will
happen to everybody's mama and dada.

Another problem is the bags under my eyes. They continue to "broaden their horizons," and someday, if death
does not come first, or if they do not end at my nose (present location) and they overtake my face to my chin, then
that will be another serious offense. I was told by a professional dermatologist that the only way to get rid of the
bags would be to "snip and tuck" around them. I say no
way is anyone going to get near my eyes with a scalpel
or whatever it is the good doctor will use to cut me up. I
prefer to keep the unflinching bags than to risk losing my
poor eyesight—even if I must with tainted pride—carry
them to my grave.

Yet another problem is facial hairs. The spikes grow
like a lawn all over my face, as if I fertilized them. I'm
surprised that they are not coming out of my mouth and
ears too. What to do? I haven't yet found a tiny lawn mower
to keep them in check. I bought a few products that were
advertised as being able to rid a face of hair; but believe

me, even though the hairs may mercifully disappear for a few days, they soon raise their nubs and antagonize me in more prickly ways.

A dermatologist advised me to shave with an actual razor, the same kind that men use. At first, I thought, how could I, as a woman, shave? I could not fathom taking a razor in hand and plying it down my face in manly dexterity, but I soon learned that if I did not do so and depend only on plucking, I would not have time for other activities, even necessary ones. Shaving, however, is a slap in my face. I became highly suspicious of the dermatologist who suggested this method. Did she want to experiment on me, try to transform a female into a male? Scientists are like that, always looking for some weird distortion to serve themselves a Pulitzer. Anyway, my previously smooth face now displays male razor bumps. I hope to sue for this.

Plucking hairs is criminal activity, because it steals time, big time. I spend hours searching for all of the stubbly hairs on my face. Worse yet, is that if I shave or pluck in the morning, by the time I reach home in the evening, some of the razed or plucked hairs have again raised their prickly heads. I fear what lengths they could reach if I have a long day at school. I cannot damage my self esteem to be dragging a full beard or mustache by day's end, which might happen soon, so I pack a razor and a tweezer in my purse and take frequent restroom breaks. Students love teachers who take frequent bathroom breaks—the longer the better for them.

Logically, however, if I have to fall back on plucking, and if plucking takes all day and then hairs grow back overnight so that I have to spend all of the following day plucking again, and this pattern repeats daily, there will be no time for grading essays, and then I'll have to retire. I'm not sure, though, that anyone sees the growth on my face because my mirror is magnified to the 15th power of the naked eye. So I hold my head high and pretend that no one sees the jutting hairs. I do, however, take precautions and steer clear of people wearing bifocals.

(Does she want to turn me into a man?)

Boldly, age spots and moles claim space on my face from time to time, but those can usually be removed periodically by the same shady dermatologist who told me to shave. The removal, however, is no sunshiny picnic. I grind my teeth, brace myself, grab on to the arm of the executioner's chair as the physician sizzles off each prominent spot with a laser "gun."

For me who have age-related spots chiseled into my DNA (my mother and grandmother had them), burning that number of spots is tantamount to open fires roasting every inch of my body.

The sad thing about this procedure, is that the spots reappear after a while, so for my face to look less like a dalmatian's, those wretched sizzles have to be repeated after several weeks, and that beat goes on. I sometimes wonder whether the dermatologist is a sadist because, for a fee, she will burn on and on and on until in gross agony, I hold up my hand for her to stop. Money, I realize can lead to perversion.

Mirrors at work have become my anathema. My mirror at home treats me more delicately and is respectful of my feelings. On the mornings before I leave for work, my home mirror transmits a reasonable picture, a picture of a healthy, vigorous woman who has eons of teaching left in her. However, in the half hour it takes me to drive to work, the mirror at work switches on me. It taunts me with a distorted picture of an older woman. It boldly reflects thinner and grayer hair, eye bags that have crept considerably lower, more and deeper wrinkles, and lips more shriveled than the ones I left at home. I could never understand how that dang mirror at work could transform the beautiful me in half of an hour—only 30 by 60 ticks of the clock. I didn't think that even 30 days could have done that to me. That mirror has been slapped repeatedly by moi (not to be broadcasted by anyone), but not in the presence of other bathroom patrons lest they think me extremely mentally agitated and call security to throw me into some godforsaken crazier institution. Anyway, I have a mind to sue the mirror manufacturers for mirror discrimination. How could the one at work show me up so much uglier than the one at home? At an institution that places numerous signs about equal opportunity for all in its most public spaces, where is that equality in mirrors?

Smart readers, be suspicious of your mirrors at work. They might be hacked to distort your lovely self and to get you to retire sooner than you intend. Examine the mirrors: look behind and around them as I have done, to make sure that they're not hooked up to any funny apparatus. If you see anything amiss, except for small crawly spiders, sue your establishment—always sue—sue repeatedly. You will need the money for retirement. The more suits you win, the more money you will accumulate for luxurious retirement.

Suing might make the difference between retiring to luxury and retiring to search for a greeter's job.

Posture

Upright posture is important for looking younger. Apart from people who develop osteoporosis or some other bone deficiency, many older people, whose backs are bending to an acute angle, may be able to correct that problem if they surround themselves with images of upright skeletons. In my case, I have young students around me to visually remind me to walk with as straight a back as possible, so when I see them, especially if they are looking my way, I throw back my shoulders, I hold up my chin, I plant my feet firmly on the ground, and I make my groovy moves. I want them to know that they have nothing over me, because I too can have as majestic a posture as they have. A perpendicular posture should be kept uppermost in mind because retirement police lurk around corners bent on reporting those who cannot unbend themselves.

I study the young ladies strutting on campus, and then I go home and practice "the walk," trying to excel at it. I draw a straight line with chalk on the floor, balance a book on my head, plaster my eyes to the wall, throw back my shoulders, and walk on the line. I wear 6" high heels, so that I might project like the young ladies with rolling backsides and protruding chests. I've also tried to sleep on the floor, so that I could straighten any bones that might be thinking of rounding off on me. One of my high school teachers advised her students to sleep on the floor for perfecting posture. At that time, I asked myself, are we in jail to sleep on the cold floor? In retrospect, I'm taking that advice. I have placed a nice quilt between me and the cold floor.

In the halls on campus, I might slump in a corner, resting and relaxing, but then a young lady with straight back would pop up, and wouldn't you know it, that would be my cue to throw back. Yes, I know how to work that picture to my advantage, and if some of my retired colleagues had been better mimics, fakes, impostors, they probably would have kept their jobs longer. My theory is fudge, fudge, fudge. I've also heard a similar theory, "Fake until you make it," so those are my guiding theorems.

When I start dragging my knuckles on the ground like a Neanderthal female, and I am so stiff that I can no longer unfold a folded back, and when I look into my trusty mirror and all of me is looking like a praying mantis, pop-out eyes and all, I will know that it is time to go home for good, and then it's *adios* for me.

Arms and Hands

Lifting weights have helped to keep enormous flab off my under arms, but I don't view arms as a huge problem because I regularly see arms that vary from colossal to bony, out in broad daylight, so the modest "meat" that hangs under my arms shouldn't be too disgusting. I don't think any student will regurgitate his or her breakfast because of them. In any case, if anyone should hurl in front of me after taking a look at my arms, I will be clued in to wearing long sleeves henceforth, but maybe a tattoo of some kind on an arm could pretty up things a bit, add some appeal and some distraction. Maybe the very popular multicolored butterfly would linger well on my biceps. It would signal that I am young at heart—liberated, a rebel, a freedom thinker, a cool person—who is in tune with herself. People don't ask cool people to leave, and that's me, cool and chic.

(Keeping up appearances)

The topsides of my hands are scaly, and bones and veins are visible to the point where they entertain me if I curl and uncurl my hands. My veins look somewhat like snakes climbing tree trunks, my bones. Some might think that they are hands that should retire. Others might think that they could improve if I went to a manicurist, but I contend, could the manicurist glue fat to them to cover up the ghastly sight? Also, for all of the 70 years that I have been on this earth, I have not been able to haul myself for an appearance at the manicurist. What is he or she going to say to me? You have terrible looking hands only so that she or he could make a few bucks off of ugliness? I will still hand-wash dishes, still scour my bathtub, still scrub my face sink, still sing "Happy Birthday" twice when I wash my hands, and still will cut my nails to their lowest point without cutting into flesh.

Manicurists have visions of dainty hands with long nails that are notorious for harboring germs; and so, they dab nail polish over the hideous, unhealthy bacteria. Shame on them. I will not be attempting to cover up germs with any variety of colors—especially black—so if anyone wants to judge me by my hands, let the one who is without germs under his or her nails do so. Hands don't tell anyone when it's time to go home, except in cases where the nerves are affected so badly that a person can no longer use one hand to calm the other long enough to perform important duties associated with the job. Most importantly is that my hands could still write terse comments on compositions, still could point at a student if needed, still could hold markers to write on the board, and still could perform every action necessary for sustaining a healthy me. If my hands become uncontrollable, dashing themselves in every direction, I'll trust my doctor to tell me that my hands cannot be rehabilitated, so I will need to park myself at home.

The Droopy

Apparently, if a woman is sufficiently endowed (the scope of this discussion cannot address various breast sizes and which directions they might take), when she gets older, her breasts gravitate towards the ground and aim to catch up with her feet. Imagine that, breasts walking way down there with feet. I was determined to find a way for this not to happen to me, so I tried the following:

Method #1: I wore bras to bed, hoping that the overtime hoisting would work, but that discomfort did not point my breasts northward one tittle.

Method #2: I cut up my bras, pieced them back together so that this time the straps were more taut, and hopefully more uplifting. Many of those bras now lay abandoned in my dresser drawer next to my undies because they did not provide the upliftment I needed.

Method #3: I pledged trust in catalogs that show droopy old women, who with the help of crisscrossed bands, could sling up their breasts and recreate a movie star figure. When I saw this, I thought this is my savior. This time, it was no crazy invention of my own, but one that was being promoted as successful, and women were buying it. Surely, if it was in a catalog and working for movie stars, it should work for me too. My hopes rode high on the "three times a charm" cliché, and I crossed my fingers, knocked on wood, and kissed my Bible. In a few weeks, however, I revoked my trust, every drop of it, when I realized that the product had no measurable success for me. My breasts were still creeping downwards. The catalogs have disappointed me—big time. When I bought the product, wore it confidently, and thought it was the product I needed all along, it was not. The mirror at work unabashedly did me in. My breasts appeared as flabby as though I had not worn the "miracle" bra. I spat and spat on that mirror more than I had done before. Expletives hung at the tip of my tongue.

When I realized sadly that bra methods #1, #2, and #3, did not work, my patience ran thin, and I was tempted to seek surgical intervention, but I wanted to be able to feed my family and myself. I love food. They love food. I live to eat; they live to eat, so I took some yoga style breaths, counted to ten, drank some filthy wine, and recomposed myself. I analyzed each method I had used to see whether I could come up with another invention, and then is when I thought of:

Method #4. Why did I not think of so obvious a plan in the first place? I hoisted my mammary glands into two hammock-like cups I cut from a specially bought D-cup to the nth power bra, slung them to the bed and retired to therapy for the night. On second thought, I will share my step-by-step method with you in case you would like to try it:

1. Cut out two bra cups from a firm new D-cup to the nth power bra. Old ones will not work after their tautness has expired.

2. On each side, make two holes, large enough to pass rope through them.

3. Loop rope through the holes on both sides of the cups.

4. Pound two carpenter sized hooks, about the distance between your two breasts (measure the space between your two breasts to get accurate measurement), into the headboard. If you do not want to damage your headboard, pound the hooks into the back of the headboard or to the wall. In fact, if you do not want to damage headboard or wall, look for suction cups that will not mar headboard or wall.

The whole contraption should resemble an inverted sling shot.

5. At night or even in the day, if you have nothing better to do, hike your breasts into the cups and sling the attached ropes to the hooks so that the cups are taut and your breasts can feel a pulling up, never, never down. If you feel any downward pull, then there is too much play on the ropes. You must get up and put some knots in those ropes to increase their tautness.

Now that you know the procedure, you might try it. You might have better success than I had, but the lyrics of "To dream the impossible dream," have always inspired me, so I'm still looking for a solution. I learned not to be too hard on myself, because I figure whoever wants to send me home for sagging breasts could attempt to do so. They will be served a gigantic law suit against breast discrimination, and tah dah, I will be awarded enough money to retire, maybe even in luxury—with yacht and summer/winter/spring/fall home—if I'm lucky.

Lower Realms

Age and the occasional slothfulness that accompanies it accelerate cellulite multiplication as my experience has taught me. That amassed cellulite makes sure that it provides me with additional embarrassment. I might be in the over 50 percentile for thickness in the waist, but a large waist is no reason for anyone to shoo me home. Below my waist is no better. My hips are broad, but with strategic angle twists, persistence, and patience, I am able to press myself through wide doors.

My legs are thick colonial pillars holding up my massive structure. My knees are so knobbly that the only way I could appear in public is by hiding them. If I win the lottery, I might seek some reductive surgical solution, but in the meantime, I will wear long skirts and pants, since like other wanna-have solutions, it might cost money that I might not be able to acquire in my natural lifetime. I am also a humpty dumpty type, prone to tumbling over myself, so it is by faith I wear the long skirts and pray I will not trip and hurt any body part so badly that the doctor will not be able to put me back together again.

For my feet I am mainly interested in whether they can take me from point "Y" to point "Z". I might indulge in prettying them up a bit with anklets and cheap nail polish on special occasions, but to have pedicurists touch my feet is out of the question. If manicurists cannot mess with my hands, then definitely pedicurists can't mess with my feet, since feet are uglier and smellier than hands. I applaud manicurists and pedicurists for inventing those ways of earning a living just like other professionals who charge more for similar prettying up, but that is one expense I will do without if I am to save for more important reasons. So, when it comes to feet, I will know it's time to retire when they refuse to plant themselves firmly enough to keep me from toppling over. That is all the prettying-up I need.

Height

Lordy, lordy, lordy, who would have thought that even someone's height could be fiddled with.

I went to the doctor's office recently, and the uppity nurse told me I was 5' 2.5".

I said, "How come I am not 5' 3" as I was the last time I was here? Is it possible for someone to shrink? I don't think so." I was sure that was logical.

She said, "Yuh think yuh getting younger?" There was a smirk on her face. I felt like slapping somebody.

I wondered whether I was eventually going to shrink so much that I would become one with the ground, and if so, how soon that would be. If rapid shrinking occurs, I will have to invent method(s) to stretch myself like a snake sizing up its prey. However, I have the following letter written, just in case the ground and I become one.

Dear Boss,

When you don't see me at work, don't wonder where I might be, and trust me, don't come looking for me, because you wouldn't want to be where I am. In fact, if you find me, that will mean that you too are a profound sinner. No doubt. You refused to raise me a few measly bucks when I deserved it. You gave me "4's" on my own self evaluations when I stressed that my work was of "5's" quality, and you jarred my nerves when you spied on me in the classroom under the pretense of executive privilege, so yes, you deserve to be here.

Tell the gossipers at work they could come visit any time, and tell the ones who said they wanted my job, and then tried to bully me out by saying I was fossilizing as in the dinosaur age that they could now have my job. With pleasure, I will send them all the students I meet down here because they are the kinds they deserve.

Professor in Hell

Weight

In old age, some people accumulate weight and find it difficult to shed excessive pounds. That is happening to me, so when I become too heavy for the elevator, or when the administration cannot provide the hydraulic lift that I might require to take me to my office on tenth floor, I will have to retire, but I will have a grin on my face because that will call for another lawsuit. The law states that reasonable accommodations should be provided for the handicapped. "Reasonable" for me is by *all* means possible, to misquote Malcolm X, but to borrow his fervor. A hydraulic lift is indeed a possibility. I have dreams of being raised, grinning in that lift, and waving to everyone below. Other faculty with physical handicaps will thank me for coming up with such a brilliant idea so that they too could requisition similar equipment.

I try to shed pounds by exercising as much as I can in my office during a break between classes. I bunch up shredded essays (Don't ask why those essays were torn. Just imagine how frustration works over ho-hum scribblings), raise my arm high, and then jerk my wrist as I aim for the trash can. Sometimes I beat my average score and then I stand and take a bow, another taxing exercise. I balance a pencil on my head and walk a straight line on the floor; I flick an eraser off of my desk into a paper cup; I ride across the room on my chair; I draw big loops in the air with my arms; I throw sharpened pencils at the bull's eye, drawn on the wall. I am still able to perform all of those strenuous exercises, but when I can no longer perform them, I will know that plenty is amiss, and I will take my last speed across the office. By then I might be so carefree that I would venture a wild ride through the hall.

(Freedom is taking a ride down the hall)

The Involuntary

When I was younger, I would have been embarrassed to mention a weak bladder, a burp, a fart, or some other scandalized function, but now, I can openly discuss these issues, so that others could be forewarned. Because of some unfair quirks (age of body parts), these perfectly healthy activities become more disgusting among seniors. Bladders get tired of holding as much urine as they did previously, linings in stomachs become diaphanous so that food cannot be digested as efficiently as previously, and organs slow down and become stretched to capacity with less buoyancy so that the poor senior's body has to pay. Actually, no one should be embarrassed about his or her involuntary bodily functions because everyone—kings, queens, presidents, prime ministers, czars, rulers, rich, poor, old, and young—has to deal with them, or they will be sick.

So, I'll say it with no frills; if ever water comes trickling down my legs while I am lecturing, I will consider that to be a serious sign to discontinue my dates in the classroom. Yes, I know of the adult diapers, etc., that businesses have been promoting, but I don't know how much I can depend on them. I do not fancy trying one out in the classroom, only to discover that it didn't work—not with the copious amount of urine my body has been manufacturing by the nanoseconds.

My nose, especially when the pollen count is at its highest, presents me with another problem. I might dig into my nostrils with tissue before class, but by the time I get to class two minutes later, a bugger(s) might form and dangle. In fact, bugger-forming is relentless and keeps up the production pace in the classroom. Turn to the chalk board and there's no bugger; turn around and there are buggers from each tunnel in the middle of my face. Same for the yellow mucus that generates out of the corners of my eyes. That ugliness appears and then reappears at will. Grossness is not what students pay for.

Sometimes, I have not been able to shut up the honks that the expelling of gas that my end system makes. Even at my boldest and most liberated moments, I am embarrassed. I try to dash behind the lectern or to back away from front-row students (God bless them. I love front-row students), shuffle my feet, slam a book on the desk, or do something noisy, so that the escaping sound is drowned, but I don't think those tactics always work. Sometimes I don't dash, slam the book, or shuffle quick enough. However, my longsuffering students want good grades, so they stifle any appearance of being privy to those honks. I love those students and feel that I should add ten points to their end-of-term scores as a bonus for having learned important life lessons—endurance, patience, forgiveness.

One thing I learned is not to carry certain types of foods for lunch. Boiled eggs, tuna, black bean, cheese sandwiches, eat them all at home. Not only will those sandwiches have me honking, but they will also be accompanied by bursts of air so foul that it would seem as though the classroom were an abattoir. Strong enough perfumes, even of the Mary Magdalene strength cannot counter the awful scents.

I have used some of the commercialized products touted to take care of that gas problem, but sometimes, when I am in dire need, they fail me. The silver lining to this problem, however, is that I hope that one of my students would have recognized my extreme dismay and will concoct an effective solution to the problem.

When the physical becomes so pathetic that I cannot drag myself out of bed, cannot shuffle to the bathroom, cannot brush my teeth, cannot scramble a breakfast egg, cannot shower, dress, dab on sufficient makeup, cannot look my trusty mirror in the eye, I will know it is time to hightail it outta the job, and I will do just that.

Mental

Remembering Schedules

SOME SAY THAT OLDER PEOPLE lose their memory, among other things such as teeth, hearing, agility, sense of humor, libido, and bladder control. I am testament to the fallible memory theory to some extent, but some of my young students tend to forget more than I do. They are notorious for forgetting when assignments are due, how to use proper grammar, how to organize an essay, how to spell, what time the class meets, where their classrooms are (At orientation, students should be given compasses so that they could always find their way to their classrooms), who is their teacher, to take off their pajamas, to brush their teeth, to comb their hair, and God knows what else the naked eye cannot behold.

Maybe a comparison of memory retention between old and young is unfair. Maybe my students have much more to remember than I do; but to be evenhanded to myself, I have to remember to wake up at 5:30 A.M. on the days I have classes, fix breakfast in keeping with the nutritionists' advice, scarf it down with minimum slopping, gulp six glasses of water, swallow a multitude of vitamins suggested for sustaining eternal life, conduct my toilet affairs, shower thoroughly, floss and brush my teeth, dress in the latest fashion, slather on layers of makeup to properly cover up my wrinkles, arrange my hair strategically to hide the bald and the gray and still be in style, disengage security alarm to my house, pick up my house key, my office key, and my car key; remember the route to my job, park in the area designated for a jalopy like mine, pick up the appropriate instructional materials from my office, put in an appearance in front of the correct class at the right time and in the designated classroom, teach the lesson of the day, remember my students' names for the roll—all of that—after remembering tons of grammatical rules; more tons of vocabulary, their meanings, spellings, origins, evolution, etc.; the Modern Languages Association's persnickety rules for presenting research; the elements of fiction, the elements of poetry, the elements of the play; multifarious figures of speech; the meanings of archetypal, modern, national and international physical and abstract symbols; literary periods and the contents of their literature; and much more—to efficiently mark their essays and other test materials, and then to remember to smile when I return their papers. I don't think the memory problem is comparable—not yet. Trust me, when I cannot remember my first name, where I live, which side of the road to drive on, or where my office is, I will no longer show up for work.

Remembering Students' Names

I'll confess that one of my biggest memory problems is trying to remember all of my students' names, but psychologists have suggestions on how to master this. One strategy that I read of was that if a person is right handed, she should look up to the right when she says the person's name. If the person is left handed, then he should look up to the left when he says the person's name, and so the right-handed me, usually looks up to the right hemisphere of heaven, as I imagine it situated in the classroom, and I supplicate with God to help me to remember my students' names. I don't know if I do not supplicate earnestly enough or what, but that strategy does not work for me. If I'm lucky, I'll remember only a handful of names on the first day of classes. Hurrah again to front-row students, because their names are the ones I am most likely to remember. Maybe, if I had only a few names to learn by looking up to the heavens, the strategy might work, but with 100 students and sometimes more every semester, some of whom do not often appear in the classroom, the task is overwhelming. To add to that, each of those students have at least two names, some of which are not in the "Smith" or "Jones" margin of difficulty.

I have another trick that aids me in remembering names and words that I cannot recall immediately. When I am trying to spit out a word and cannot regurgitate it at the very moment I need it, I begin with "A" and hurry through to "Z," straining to think of the person or the word I need, and fishing to find the letter that the person's name or the word begins with; sometimes, just like magic—bam—the word or name pops into my brain, and delightful juices flow and flow onto my hippocampus, elated with its success. Recently, I've been having to call up that technique more often, and sometimes, if you notice me a little tipsy, it might be from the copious flow of juices on my brain. Brain juice is delicious.

I tried to use another technique that psychologists recommend: the association technique. They say that I should associate a student I am meeting for the first time with another person, place, event, or thing. Because this suggestion is wide open to various kinds of associations, I tried each of them with the earnest intention of ensuring 100 percent success. First, I tried the "person" association. I tried pairing each incoming student with a famous celebrity, a president, a previous student, or with another one in that class, or in any of my other classes. "Notorious villain" was held back only for a dire situation. Pairing worked to some extent. I tended to use personality traits such as the comical student with a comedian, the bombastic with a politician, the grandiloquent with a preacher, the fashion fiasco with a diva. Sometimes physical traits such as resemblance, height, carriage, mannerisms, grin and so forth, helped me to make the memorable associations and led me to remembering some students' names.

Next, I tried the "place" association. Even though, I did not find that any of my students resembled a continent or an island or any geographical formation, I was able to remember some for their Mount Everest hair-dos. I associated some with where they sat in class every day. That was a big help. The names of front-row students seemed easiest to remember, but that did not always work. Sometimes, I was more likely to remember the back row shy person, the middle row comedian, or the second row smartest student I ever had. In that way, place became significant.

Place also helped when a student from a specific region, country, or island spoke or dressed in accordance with the place that he or she hailed from. U.S. northerners always boasted that they were better dressers than southerners, although southerners insisted that they were more genteel than their northern counterparts. Some insisted on appearing in nothing less than name brand garbs, while others wore whatever they culled. Shoes were sometimes fancy and expensive or flip flops were on the shabbier end.

Sometimes it was the diction or the accent that helped me to remember a person. I didn't have many British students, but I had several from the Caribbean, whose early education was influenced by the British and whose spelling and pronunciation tended to be like the British, so place helped when it came to peculiarities of speech, spelling, diction, and dress.

Next, I tried the "event" association. I assumed that the "event" category referred to a memorable occasion such as a Michael Jackson concert, a President of the United States' inaugural banquet, a visit to the moon, an encounter with an angel/devil, or the likes of someone performing at or attending those events with whom I could pair my students. I failed miserably with those elaborate events.

It was more reasonable to associate my students with the few school activities I attended. Which professor with piles of essays to grade has time for a walloping number of school events? I think I remembered football students fairly well—not because of their fame on the field or so, but because they towered over and around me. I didn't want to be crushed by one of those tractor-sized guys, so yes, I remembered their names so that I could keep my social distance. Others performed in plays, choirs, band, cheer leading, debate teams, writing contests, and so forth, so I was able to associate some with their activity.

The only technique left for me to try was to associate my students with things. "Things" is the most maligned, least helpful, vaguest word in any language that could account for almost every spec of matter in this world wide web of a world. Should I associate a student with an animal, a fish, a book, a flower, a pot spoon? Remember, I have students' essays to grade and cannot go down my roll of 100 students trying to figure out an apt "thing" that would match a student. For me, that would be counterproductive. What if a student is a pot spoon today and evolves into a strainer tomorrow? I cannot risk that weirdness of associating students with things. I find a modicum of success by remembering and identifying students with what they wrote about in their essays (a thing)—whether it was something positive or negative, stimulating or boring (because I cried over those).

Remembering Spellings

Along with trying to remember students' names, another memory problem is occurring because some students consistently misspell words. After repeatedly seeing the misspellings, I sometimes doubt myself; is it a lot or alot, every day or everyday, everyone or every one, referred or refered, cinnamon or cinammon, even though or eventhough, amend or ammend, necessary or neccesary, and many others. Thank God I own a dictionary, and in most cases will recognize the "funniness" of the spelling, so I can look it up.

Recognizing Legitimate Vocabulary

Not only does an occasional spelling give me problems, but also the words that are being surreptitiously added to the dictionary. Some words that were once brutally maligned as slang/informal/colloquial/substandard or otherwise, are now knighted as honorable/acceptable/ utilitarian/ proper. Standard American English is undergoing erosion, similar to what has been caused by climate change.

Many of the new words pertain to technology; I confess that I know only a smattering of technical jargon, so I readily claim ignorance of those. The ones that boggle my mind are the curse words, even though I already knew most of them; vulgarities, and slang now jostle proudly among other established words in our official lexicon. For example, the following new words are only a few out of sometimes thousands that are added almost every day. Many of these words creep onto the world wide web overnight. How am I, a person who needs sleep like other normal people, to know that these new words wormed themselves into our lexicon overnight? It's no longer like traditional dictionaries that were revised every five years and gave us time to memorize them—the whole dictionary. Any so-called word that did not appear in that tome was substandard. What's alarming is that even my computer underlines some of the new words as nano words; so with a brain that is less competent than a computer, how am I to know that the following words slipped into the *online urban dictionary* and do not deserve a "no such word" comment on a student's paper?

Biatch (noun): Used as an affectionate or disparaging form of address. The familiar word, "Bitch," is now dressed up to look like a lady.

Brewer's droop (noun): Inability in a man to achieve or maintain an erection as a consequence of excessive alcohol intake. Where is the term to describe the lack of libido in a woman due to excessive alcohol intake? Doesn't gender bias mean anything anymore? If a new word is invented for a male function, shouldn't a corresponding female term be added also?

Bromance (noun): A close nonsexual friendship between men. That word is deceptive. Because it contains the word, "romance," anyone trying to decipher its meaning might think that it is referring to gay relationships, and again, where is the corresponding female term? Sismance?

Craptacular (adjective): Remarkably poor or disappointing. "Crap," the noun was not disparaging enough. Will the comparitive be more craptacular and its superlative, most craptacular?

Drunk text (noun): A text message sent while drunk, typically one that is embarrassing or foolish. How about drunk tweet? Does a person have to be drunk to send one that is embarrassing, doltish, insulting? That question has been answered repeatedly.

Fist bump (noun): A gesture in which two people bump their fists together, as in greeting or celebration. A handshake transmitted too many germs, so smart people came up with a way to convey fewer germs. Why not make contact even less contaminating with a finger click at each other or with the respected "namaste" between indians?

Ghost (verb): to abruptly cut off all contact with someone, such as a friend or former romantic partner, by no longer accepting or responding to phone calls, instant messages, etc. Up to this time, "Ghost" was a noun, so for grammarians it is difficult to think of a "A ghost ghosting."

Listicle (noun): An article consisting of a series of items presented as a list. Why is "list" suddenly irksome to journalists?

Prosopagnosia (noun): An inability to recognize faces. I suppose that other five-syllable disease-sounding terms exist for the inability to recognize places, things, names, etc.

Sausage fest (noun): An event or group in which the majority of participants are male. What will they create to describe an event with mostly females? Try it. See what you come up with. Grapefruit, melon, apple fest?

Side-eye (noun). A side-long glance or gaze, especially when expressing scorn, suspicion, disapproval, or veiled curiosity. To convey this very meaning I previously used "evil eye" to mean the same thing, but maybe with a greater degree of meanness.

Truther (noun): One who believes that the truth about an important subject or event is being concealed from the public by a powerful conspiracy. I suppose people who believe that scientists/government is not telling what they know about aliens would be called truthers.

Woo Woo (adjective): Dubiously or outlandishly mystical, supernatural, or unscientific. "Crazy" was too decent, unimaginative, tempered? This sounds like the first expression my eight-month grandson would use to call his dad.

Yas! (exclamation): Expressing great pleasure and ex-citement. Even my know-it-all computer flagged that as a non-existing word. In fact, it flagged most of the words in this list. What happened to eureka! OMG!!!! or just plain !!!!!!?

Yowza! (interjection): Used to express surprise or amazement. This word is too similar to Yas! But it adds to our word choices.

So when my students write "hoeish," "gonna," "wanna," "confusement," "darkful," "conversate" and others that they regard as "words," I wonder whether the insouciance of the world wide web messed with my brain while I slept, and whether I should mark those "words" as incorrect on their papers. I also wonder that if the specific word/slang/col-loquialism, etc., is not on the web today, would it be there tomorrow? Should I resist my "no such word" comment because of its anticipated value? Its potential?

I wouldn't want to discredit a word only to discover next morning that voila, it's a part of our lexicon. Then the big old joke will be on me. Students would broadcast that their English teacher does not know her vocabulary. Ever heard of an English teacher not knowing the meaning of a word? Students consider that to be a sin incarnate, and no English teacher should be in front of any class if she does not know the meaning of a word. All of this is not good for my students' evaluations, and can cause the ultimate death of my career.

Learning Abbreviations

Also, abbreviations and acronyms in text messages are constantly being created.

There are multitudes of important and not-so-important acronyms that I do not know the meanings of. When this new age litany of text inventions took place, it was a bit much for me. For instance, after I gave my students a collaborative (a collusion of sorts) assignment, just when the assignment was due, a young lady complained that her partner was not contributing to the project. She showed me the text message from her partner. "LMFAO about that project."

How was I to know that that was a derogatory term? I thought the text was in the same spirit of LOL, the one acronym I had seen, but then she enlightened me and said that it meant Laughing My Fat Ass Off. How am I to know when some of these terms are being pulled out of a magician's top hat? Who are the magicians, and who authorizes them to create new words, new terms? From what my googling revealed, there are over 1,501 text abbreviations, enough to create a dictionary of its own, and enough to send me into a tizzy.

To manage my ignorance, I am no longer accepting text messages from my students as legitimate communications, especially the grammatically incorrect ones such as YOLO—You Only Live Once. I try to tell my students that the "only" in this acronym is a misplaced modifier, and that since "only" refers to "once," it should be placed close to "once," and that it should read, You Live Only Once. Of course, who am I—one humble ignoramus—to overrule what multitudes have been displaying on tee shirts, hats, tattoos, and all kinds of places? They seem to think that I have no right interfering with what has been condoned by multitudes of smart users. I almost got spit balls thrown at me for suggesting this in class.

(We want YOLO!!!)

With all of these changes to our lexicon, modern English is becoming my new second language that I'll have to learn to keep abreast of.

Hemming and Hawing at Social Gatherings

Some of my friends and family are skeptical about my ability to teach, and they say, retire. Oftentimes, my memory at social gatherings does not serve me as well as when I am in the classroom. When I am with friends and family, I stumble over words, and sometimes I go batty—spaced out—searching for the very word I need, but I cannot be blamed if those words elude me at those times because I might have intelligent ideas on my mind.

Some do not recognize that I am socially inept, as awkward as a pig on a water slide. I am not always (sometimes, however, I can go over and beyond) very effective when chattering over trivial, everyday tit bits. Chit-chattering is not my style, so, when I behave like a fish out of water and I run dry or go blank, and they call me a bloke, it may not transfer to my job—sometimes maybe, but not often. I am not a schizo, but different people and different situations bring out different me's; the stumbling, bumbling me is often on display in social situations, especially when I feel pressured to speak wisdom as King Solomon. Some people think that teachers know everything; however, to heck with them because to me, being socially correct is not as important to me as being correct in the classroom.

I have to be sufficiently alert to be able to point out the multitude of problems that I come across in students' writings. If the wheels in my brain stop cogitating and I can no longer detect these problems, I will know, and I promise, I will pack up and go home. I will then have time to write my obituary, air brush a photo to accompany it, plan my funereal party—menu, flowers, music, DJ, invitations, guest list, decorations, and every exciting fun detail that accompanies funeral planning.

Social

Fun with Grandkids

MY FRIENDS TELL ME TO go home to my grandkids. "You will have plenty fun with them. They will keep you looking young," is what they say.

"Indeed," I say, "If haggard and tired also mean young and fun, then I will have plenty of that." I've had many summer, spring and Christmas breaks to assess the situation and to know what I will be up against.

In the mornings the kids wake up too early, and in the evenings they go to bed too late for me to enjoy other than "Sesame Street," "Arthur," "Peppa Pig," and of course, "Curious George," and other age-discriminating TV shows. I would prefer my age-discriminating shows such as "As the World Turns," "The Young and the Restless," "Judge Judy," "The Maury Show," and others. When I sigh with boredom over their shows, they say, "Blessed are the Merciful for they shall see God," and they sit on my legs so that I can't move to change the channel, not even if a doomsday event such as earthquake, flood, hurricane, epidemic, pandemic, volcano or other earthshaking phenomenon is erupting and there is breaking news on the TV.

I prepare healthy meals for the three kids. When I put the delicious gourmet-looking meal on the table in front of them, they eye me as though I am about to crucify them; and because they have no respect for the food, it becomes major missiles to aim at each other and at me too. "Splat, got you," the two-year old said when she threw the boiled pumpkin in my face.

I wave my index finger from side to side and I adopt a mean look. "Say you're sorry, dear," I try to teach good manners. This one is too little to give a mean spank, so I have her hold out her hand and slap (as a patty cake slap) it with the hope that she will understand that worse could come if she continues that behavior.

"Sorrrryy?" The word draaaags out, and then it is splat again and laughter, not even a smothered docile "heh, heh, heh" but an outright open-mouth "hah, hah, hah" explodes from the 2-year old, her three-year-old, and five-year old brothers. Now, I have to tolerate a chorus of "heh, heh, heh, ha, ha, ha."

"You will be punished for this," I say and I wag my finger and move close to their eyes to make sure that they are not blind to the energy in my pointy. I have to think up punishment that will teach them not to be so mean and that will keep the Child Protective Service from knocking at my door.

"Gramma, you look sooo funny," the three-year old laughs. "Look in the mirror." I still have yellow smatterings on my nose.

"Let me clean your face, Grammy," the five-year old says, and his dimples blossom.

I go closer, thinking this is redemption for the brats, that their contrition is forthcoming. But then the five-year old spits on a napkin and invites the other two to spit hard on the same napkin. "We need plenty spit. Grammy has a biiiig face."

When I see the intention, I say, "No, no, that is dirty. You're not putting that on my face," and I run to the sink to douse water over my face. No way do I want communal spit on my face.

My heart cries and sinks and sinks again, dejected over the best efforts I put into creating appetizing dishes, with designs, flavors, and colors that I carefully arrange on their plates. I create roosters with green spinach bodies, orange cockscombs from carrots, and blue eyes with blueberries. On another day, I might make bear-shaped egg sandwiches, peanut butter and jelly volcanoes, or string-bean-shaped snakes, but the brats never see my art—only whether the food suits their tastes or not. Tastes can vary widely between three brats.

They say they want to take **me** to the ice cream parlor so that I could learn about good food. It so happens that the ice cream parlor is also my favorite place, but guess who's taking whom. Yes, it's me taking them, because I have to drive, and I have to pay. The scrooges will not offer to open their piggy banks—not even once—in the name of fair play, to pay for their ice cream. Anyway, I take them, pay, and settle in to enjoy my treat. Unbeknownst to me, they are gobbling down their ice cream so that they could grab mine while distracting me; after the sinners steal my ice cream, they smile sweetly and tell me that **I** am sharing and that the Bible says "Blessed are those who share." It took me awhile, but I am now privy to every grab-my-ice-cream trick they could think up, so I hold tight to my ice cream, and threaten to break their piggy banks and drain them, if they try to grab my ice cream one more time. I wag my finger at them and display my meanest look.

They stick out their tongues at babies in strollers passing by; the babies' parents stare at me, and I wish I were ice cream melting and that no one could see me with them. What should I do with these children? I wish I had a reasonable disclaimer I could wear in giant letters around my neck. Maybe if it just said, "GRANDMA" people might understand the proverbial approach that grandparents are allowed to spoil their kids and it is the parents who are truly responsible for disciplining them.

We go for a stroll in the neighborhood, and they skip ahead of me so that my lack of friskiness could be in full display in front of their neighbors. They call out, "Gramma, do this," while they jump and run. "C'mon, Gramma; get some exercise. C'mon, c'mon. You don't want to be called a sloth. Do you Grammy?"

They do not realize that if I pranced like them, I might have a serious broken-bone problem on the road, but no, their objective is to shame me, big time. They want to get their grimy, little fingers on the "Help. I've fallen-and-can't-get-up" button on the string around my neck. The five-year-old says, "We want to see if it really works like on TV, Grammy."

"No way. Not over my dead body. The emergency people will pick you up instead and take you to the police for committing the major crime of false alarm." I feel constrained to use drastic scare tactics because these three heads seem too stubborn for me. "You will have to stay in jail until your mom and dad could get a million dollars to bail you out, which you know they don't have." I rub it in some more. "In that case, you might have to stay in jail forever and ever and ever."

To have an ambulance, blasting its woo, woo, woo in the neighborhood, and to have neighbors gawking at the spectacle of me sprawled on the pavement cannot be entertainment to sane children. I wonder whose DNA they inherited. Not mine.

(Sprawled granny becomes a spectacle.)

Another source of persecution is when they say, "Let's go swim, Gramma," in mellifluous voices, but when I get into the pool, they pour water that has been chilled with ill-gotten ice cubes all over me.

"Stop, stop, stop," I shout in my most menacing tone, and I shake my pointy finger so vigorously that they would realize that I mean business. You would think that at their ages they would understand the seriousness of an adult's pointy finger, but they can't, for they continue to rain the frigid water over me.

I wave two pointy fingers at them.

They say I'm not a sport because players douse their coaches with buckets of ice after they win their games and the coaches laugh and enjoy it. "I am not a coach today, I was not ever a coach, and I will never be a coach," I shout to them.

"Ok. You might like to be a fish, Gramma." The six hands try to pull me under the water.

"No, no, no. No coach, no fish, nothing." They might drown me, so I stand back—way back. "No more ice cream if you touch me." My pointy finger is at them again.

They hide my makeup, take pictures of me without makeup, and with sticky, little fingers forward my pho-tos to all the social media outlets they can access on their mother's phone. The pictures carry the caption, "Grammy loses mind and wears no makeup." Then they want me to search for my own makeup. "Let's play the 'hot-and-cold game,' grammy. You'll love this game. When you get close to your makeup, we'll yell 'hot'; when you are far away, we'll yell 'cold'," the five-year-old instigator says.

My blood begins to boil, because my makeup is the only thing that renders me a bit presentable; without it, those scallywags will say I look like a cockroach, a rat, a worm, a scorpion, an armadillo—whatever ugly creature they could think up—and they threaten to disown me.

"Go ahead," I say. My secret desire is for them to do just that. I don't think it would be the first grandma divorce.

They also paint their faces with my makeup. Red eyebrows, green lips, blue noses, purple eyelids, whatever, but they do not open their piggy banks to reimburse me for new makeup. Sometimes that makeup is used to paint the dog's face, or they paint a face on the dog's behind. The dog loves the attention and the tickle on its behind, so it stands still, and they clap their hands in glee. The neighbor's free-roaming cat returns home with various colors on its paws, whiskers, and God knows where. They tackle the poor animal while it snoozes in the shade under a tree. Shoes, bed spreads, dishes, walls, all kinds of objects have been redressed with my makeup. Sometimes, however, the joke is on them because without my makeup, I am not going to any ice cream parlor.

(Happy doggy; Happy kitty)

They ball up chewed chewing gum (I've given them a kind that's touted to be healthy, so that I could have some peace while they are chewing their cuds). They say they will glue me down when I say I'm leaving. I tell them to try it, because I know that the chewed gum will not hold me down. When they discover that I cannot be glued down, they think of experimenting on gluing down something smaller—the neighbor's cat—the same one with its picture on the lamp post claiming to be lost. They will glue the cat in a box in their backyard for a day, and then they will march the cat back to the neighbor, so that they could claim reward money—money that will bring them a never ending supply of ice cream, lollipops, cup cakes, and candy.

When it is time to go to bed, they hide in crawl spaces that I cannot squeeze myself into to pull them out. By the time I wiggle them out, I am so tired that I fall asleep on the floor until they torture me with age-old tricks of stuffing my nose with toilet paper, painting my face with markers, and squeezing tubes of cold toothpaste, yes, it came from the refrigerator, on to my cheeks. And then they roar with delight when I am electrified into springing up from the chilled toothpaste. "We didn't know you could be so lively, Grammy," the three-year old says.

The five-year old gets smart, "Yes, Grammy. Did you know you might win a race in the Olympics? You're fast." He screws his face.

When those everyday tricks become monotonous, they resort to tying me to bed posts with their jump ropes. In the morning I awake with a sore back and a bitter disposition. They? Giggling, despite the threatening look on my face and my pointy fingers—both fingers. My hypothesis: they are ganging up to murder me.

To prolong the bedtime torture, on the nights that I am not tied, they would request bedtime stories—one for each of them—even when they see my drooping eyelids. I was kind with the stories. I thought I could educate them a little by including stories of repentance, generosity, kindness, and wisdom, but that has backfired big time. For instance, I am now, "Scrooge" after telling them the decent Christmas story. I told them the story of a hungry soldier going to a village and tricking the villagers into making him a healthy, hearty "stone" soup when they wanted to hide their food from him because of the war that was ongoing. Of course, the next time I made soup for them, I found three stones at the bottom of my bowl of soup. I thought that they should be told the story of the three little pigs and the Big Bad Wolf that is a part of every child's education. When I told the story, the five-year-old ring leader accused me of writing the story just to call them pigs (I have used this term to refer to their negligence to clean up their rooms). To prove that I did not write the story, I bring a copy of the story from their own library and show them that a lady wrote the story in 1922, before I was even born. "Oh no, you wrote the story," becomes the five-year-old's mantra, and the usual trio starts, "Gramma is a BBW, Gramma is a BBW" with three pointy fingers in my face. No amount of reasoning could keep them from calling me the BBW.

I now take revenge and tell them stories about Frankenstein, the Loc Ness Monster, and The Invisible Man to scare their heads under the covers. When they scream, I quit because I do not want their parents coming after me. They might shame me for my dirty get-even-with-their-innocent-kids tactic. They work all day and do not understand how age and grossly mischievous kids do not mix.

If I threaten to leave, as I often do, then woe is me. I am called Wimpy Granny, Grammy of the namby-pamby, crybaby Grandma, and then they proceed to hide my shoes, my makeup, my clothes, and my suitcase. Sometimes they will try a softer approach. Angelic smiles will miraculously appear on their faces, and they will kneel with clasped hands and imploring faces in front of me. I tell them to get themselves up because I know it is only fake repentance that will vanish if I relent. Worst of all, their mother is pregnant again. I Gotta go.

Their parents thank me for doing such a good job, but they are too busy to discover the devilish torture those cherubic faces create for me, and I, I just say, "You are very welcome. Any time, my dears," but my slothful self takes speed.

Do I want to retire from my day job and go home to that? No way. At school my students and colleagues respect me to some extent; at home, the scenario is different—I get zero respect. Roger Dangerfield, God rest his soul, should be thanked for putting a version of his meaningful "I get no respect," into my head.

Romance at Home

Another virtue that my friends possess is love. They are Romeos and Juliets, cupids carrying arrows, Venuses, Aphrodites. They think they are doing me great good by advising, "Go home to your husband. He is waiting for you with open arms. You will have a second honeymoon." They clap their hands in delight and broaden their smiles. "Maybe even a renewing of vows!" That is stretching the idea too far for my stomach, but my friends love a party.

OOOPS, my stomach cannot handle it. I suddenly feel like vomiting. I suppose they imagine that my husband and me are two "peas in a pod," enjoying romantic cruises, holding hands all day long, gazing into each other's eyes with devotion, dining and dancing at posh restaurants, stealing kisses at stunning sunsets, and God knows what else.

They, I think, have watched too many movies and TV commercials starring retired couples with hand in hand, and forced grins upon their faces. They forget that those people get paid, handsomely, I imagine, to plaster a proper smile upon their faces. Whatever their influence, they see only positive outcomes from my retiring to my husband, even though, some of them are seasoned divorcees. Bejabbers! I think and do not begrudge them their fanciful ideas, but they have to be able to winnow fact from fiction.

Suppose my husband, who retired a few years ago, isn't eager to share the space that he hogged to himself daily, while I continued to work? Has anyone of my invigilators ever considered that? I am not the same lovely young lady he married. Who's to prove that his hormones aren't still raging like my younger male students who prefer beauty over brain? Upright, flexible posture over rigidly bent and unbending structure? Seductress over school marm? Wealthy, sophisticated dowager over poor, messed-up professor? Not because he is now old and bent does it mean that his appreciation for the young and frisky has changed. No, no, no. Old and ugly do not equal love.

Of course, the world has seen many an older man trash his shriveled wife for youth and beauty, and that is even when he is ordered to pay millions in alimony. He cliches "Money is no object," to the pleasure of a new wife. He thrives on newness—new cars, new homes, new jets, new scenery and scenarios, new clothes, new jewelry, etc., so why not new wife? Sometimes the wife has sacrificed her personhood, to try to hold the family together, to define what family means, but he doesn't care. He wants frisky, so frisky he will get. To not discriminate, some women have done the same, and worse, but who's to say that my husband is not included in that high percentile of men who will leave old and ugly for new and young?

(Wow! Look at that!)

And then for him to see a wrinkled face 24/7? Who wants that? It's not like a painting that one buys and then later tires over admiring it, so shoves it out of sight under the bed. Into the closet. Sells it at a yard sale, or trashes it. I will not be pushed under the bed, or locked in a closet, so my ugliness is a get-up-in-the-morning and lie-down-in-the-evening torment in his face—every—living—day.

Not only are my wrinkles countless, but I am also several sizes larger than when we were courting. Would he mind having a hippo-sized me in his space every day? To have the hippo go to work and allow him free range over time is different from the hippo at home, sucking up his oxygen and private space.

When I retire, I will have to prepare more meals for his highness. Over the years, my cooking has not come close to earning a blue ribbon at even the remotest of country fairs, and his lord, who is finicky about the tiniest morsel that goes into his mouth, and who has become paranoid, is he going to cry "foul" and claim that I am trying to poison him? Is he going to call the cops for me? He is known for making big claims. He claimed that the neighbor's pet cockroach bit him and gave him rabies; that the neighbors' wives were smitten by his charm and wanted him to visit them, in their homes—while their husbands were at work; that he is more handsome than Elvis, could sing and gyrate better than him; and the list of outrageous claims does not end there. Will he claim that my cooking is poison? Will he sue me? I might get into big trouble—sentenced to jail—but maybe—maybe there might be more peace for me in jail than in the house, so I might not mind at all.

His wimpishness is magnified in my presence. Whenever he passes by me, he laments, "Oh godogodogod," as if he is in agony—dying—but as soon as someone, especially if it's a female, calls him on the phone, or is in his presence, even if it is for business, he immediately becomes charming, and all infirmities evaporate—pshoot—just like helium out of a balloon. "Hi, Honey, your voice is as musical as an angel's. My x-ray vision tells me that you are more beautiful than Miss Universe." I can't stand his sudden change of tone and language.

His flattery for other women has no boundaries. We go to a restaurant, "Hi Honey. You are more beautiful than Miss Universe. Will you be free for dinner? I have a seat right here for you," and he pats the space between us.

I force a broad smile at the unarmed younger ladies. I do not want them to feel as uncomfortable as I feel.

The old goat brazenly flirts in my presence, so I have learned to stay home with a good book and tell him, "Go to the hell restaurant and enjoy yourself." I add, "old man" beneath my breath.

Because of my interest in the use of language and its effect on people, I could have been tempted to go along with him. I would have liked to observe and to be titillated at which words he would select to pair with which other ones, and then the order he would string them in to arrive at some funny flattering sentence. I would have liked to see whether there would be some physical transformation on the person he was speaking to, but my adventure would be futile because he repeatedly uses his time worn predictable cliches. I could dramatize the scene with the dialogue at home and create more entertainment for me.

The waitresses want hefty tips, so they humor him for his youthful look. "You still got it in you, Sir," they say. If I had to earn my living that way, I would have done the same and maybe even looked up some flattering vocabulary to use on him.

He claps his hands in pure delight. "Yes, Honey. Yes. I have more youth in me than all those upcoming whippersnappers."

They don't know that he sports a toupe and gleaming gold teeth; that he stuffs his pants, back and front, with wash rags; plasters on more makeup than me, which will amount to tons; and dons multitudes of fake gold bands on ten fingers. I prefer that he bask in his glory without me, because I might upchuck a good dinner in the presence of decent people.

He tests me to see how I might react if he were seriously ill, which he already is, but not as much as in a physical sense as in a mind-rocking-out-of-the-sky sense. His ultimate test for me is that if he were dying and in dire need of assistance to clean his butt, would I do it for him? I can't guarantee that I will pass that test.

He thinks I should follow his orders, so he tries to adjust my behavior—like a dog trainer would correct a dog. He would like to say to me, "cook," and I will cook. "Bring me the bedpan," and I will support his laziness by running for the pee pot so that he does not have to raise his royal highness self out of bed.

To illustrate, two months ago, while I was making the beds, I hear, "Mom, mom, come quick. Come quick!"

You would think that a man who has a college degree would know after fifty years of constant reminding that his wife is not his mother. "A wife," I tell him, "cannot tolerate what a mother can. There is a biiiiig difference. My name is Meena and my parents gave me that name to be used. Use it eh." Sometimes I think he must have bought his degree from an offshore university if he cannot understand that "wife" does not equal "mother."

Pissed as usual over his hardheadedness, I go. I recognize that his voice is suddenly not as strong, not as robust, not as rowdy as it usually is, but it is his fake voice, small, distant, and heavy with manipulation. "I'm having a high, high fever. Bring the thermometer. You might have to take me to the hospital." He has never wanted me to touch our car.

I have repeatedly reminded him, "This is the U.S. of A., not a country where women are not allowed to drive." How can I suddenly drive in this emergency if he never wants me to practice?

Now that he is in trouble, this is spectacle I have to see. "Yeeeaah, I could drive you." I keep my curiosity subdued, on the down low.

Suddenly, this is code red to him. "You drive me? I don't want to die yet." His face is twisted and his eyes are squinted.

I have to push this issue up a notch while he is in dire straits, or I might never be able to drive freely, "But you just said you wanted to go to emergency. See what happens? If I can't practice, how will I drive when I need to? You will have to let me use the car."

"Nah, just put an ice pack on my head for now. I don't think this is a real emergency after all. We will call an ambulance if we need to, because I am not riding with you. Yuh think I want to die already? You don't know how to drive and that's that." He pulls the pillow over his head.

He thinks he has held me back from driving, but I laugh, a big laugh—inside—because I have my license, and my Mercedes Benz is parked at a friend's house. Take that, I say in my head, and in the kitchen I have a proper belly laugh like my insides would pop out.

I take the ice pack to his room, and I place it lightly—very lightly—on his forehead, a bit guilty after my big laugh. "Oh, you too rough. Gimme."

I give it to him. He shoves it back to me. He sees that his arm is too short to reach, "Put it on the back of my head—easy, easy, easy—no funny move." He is talking to "Rover." Ordering it what to do.

I place the pack at the back of his head. "Do you want me to get you a pillow so that you could lie on it?"

"What? It too hard for you to stand there and hold it on my head? Okay, if it's so hard for you to do a little thing for me, bring the pillow." He pretends to be losing control of his arms as he flails them excessively in the direction of the pillow.

Glad for this relief, I take the pillow to him, but my nerves are so strained that I'm cursing the gentle, fluffy article now. I'm calling it a damned pillow, because first he wants me to fluff it one way and then the other, put it behind his head and then on the side of his head. Bring him a fresh ice pack and a glass of cold water. The water is too cold; next time, it is too warm. Make some chicken noodle soup. It is too salty. It does not have enough chicken in it to be called chicken soup. He wants a higher bed. He wants a thicker blanket.

My head is spinning. My blood pressure is rising. I bring a dinner bell, "Ring it if you need me." I scoot faster than lightning, hoping to settle in the chaise lounge I bought many years ago but could not enjoy because of the many essays to grade. I have had a recurring dream that I will relax in that lounger when I retire. I will settle my derriere into the depths of that couch with a huge bowl of vanilla ice cream, hot fudge topping, mixed nuts, whipped cream, cherry on top, and mesmerizing book. But before said derriere could touch forbidden couch, I hear an insistent bell.

"Mom, mom, mom. Come, come, come." He is dying this time.

I know better. I take my time and wish that he had not left his previous girlfriends, but I am to be blamed for that. When they said he was theirs, the usually reticent me spoke up, "No, the man is mine. He loves me." I thought I was getting priceless treasure. At first, he was a gentleman, respectful, chivalrous, and as handsome as Elvis (with spit-slicked curl in middle of forehead), but over the years, beyond my understanding, he became cantankerous, angry, obstinate, selfish, and whittled down to a puny little being. I wish one of his former girlfriends could show up now and take him away. I will give her the Mercedes Benz I parked at my friend's house, my house and land, all of the money I saved for retirement, and all of the fake jewelry he gave me.

I already mapped out my plan. I will prepare the most appealing sign—HUNGRY—for panhandling if I give away everything, and I will anchor myself at an upscale shopping center—not any place too humble where people might not have money or wouldn't be walking out the store without food. I figure that no human with sufficient food in his or her shopping cart, will pass up the opportunity to drop a penny into my bucket or offer me a fruit or can of soup.

If only I had ESP when I first saw that handsome young looker, and had been able to divine from the gods, the witches, the obeah men, the voodoo priestesses—whoever—what my future would be I would not have been such a damned fool to be in this situation. I would have let that man go as quickly as a tornado passing through Kansas City.

"The pillow is flat. It needs fluffing." I feel like fluffing it on his face, but I pull it out, cuff it some blows, and shove it back into the very same spot. My ice cream is melting, so I make another leap towards it and settle in. It keeps me sane.

If I have to go to the grocery, he will time me—one hour. If I run over his allotted time, I will hear of it. "What take you so long? Yuh went to see yuh man?"

I shake my head because I often hear of this invisible man that is waiting around the corner—waiting, waiting—just for as soon as I put my head out of the door to come to me. If I text a friend or talk on the phone, it has to be that I am talking to "my man." I heard somewhere that as a man thinketh in his heart, so is he, and now I can bear witness of that.

There are an overabundance of challenges, like he is running a government. Not one word could fall out of my mouth without opposition, a big to-do, a blow up. Some days he doesn't want me to go to work because he has a headache, which of course, I cannot cure. "I have students waiting at school for me. I can't let them down. I said I was giving them a test today. I must go today." I take him an aspirin and water.

"Always students waiting, waiting on you. Like you important. They more important than me? They your husband? Damned you, woman."

"Damn you," I say beneath my breath, because he does not understand the meaning of dedication and he is toying with my allegiances.

My friends possibly assume that in addition to the charm he displays for them, and his claim that he holds a Ph.D. means that he has learned how to be broad-minded, logical, and human; but to equivocate a diploma or a title with effective education and decency would be faulty in his case. Classes at school are not always equal to class at home.

Even when I want to visit my own dear mother, he must come first. He immediately divines the Bible and says, "God says you must forsake all others and cling to your husband." For the umpteenth time, the contents of my stomach come close to hurling. He can't talk like that when it comes to my mother. I swear I will draw the line.

This time I hope he understands the full intent of what I have to say, because it is direct, simple, but loaded with threat, "Slavery is done and gone. I am not your slave to have to obey you." I do not have more to say, only to do. After fifty years, I am still trying to pound that I am not a slave into his head. He does not listen. His skull is impenetrable.

His brain is not wired like other reasonable brains, so I am taking things into my own hands—at last. Even after I retire, as long as there is breath in me, I will be looking for a post retirement job, getting out of that house and maintaining my sanity. I think that greeting people at doors is a high calling, one I will envy.

My friends don't live in my house, so they don't know of the realities. The man is charming with them, opening doors, and holding umbrellas over them, promising them that he will cook them the dinner of their lifetimes, one to die for, that he will bring them chocolates of the oh so expensive quality, that he will show up with roses rosier than their lips, and on and on and on; so I can't blame them if they are drawn to him. I wouldn't mind if he went to one of their houses and got lost, never to return to my house.

Sometimes I am tempted to flip up his toupee in front of the ladies. Just a quick, slick lift before he could realize what is taking place. That just might suggest to them that there could be other things lurking undercover in other places that they don't know of. Some men (some women too—not to be prejudiced) are put on earth to create a balance between reasonable and unreasonable, and if my friends have no paradigm for divining the subtleties of character, then they will judge only by what they see on the outside. I can't fault them, however, for being as clueless as I was and for allowing charm, chivalry, and clout to smash them in the heart as it did to me.

I have tried my best to be a mind reader because that is what his highness wants of me. I should know when to speak, when to shut up; whether he wants chicken or fish for dinner, whether there is too much butter on his toast, whether he wants his coffee black or with cream, whether, whether, whether this or whether, whether that, that or this, this or that; but try as hard as I could, I have not succeeded in understanding the conundrums of his brain.

In addition, I can't blame my friends when they think they are giving me good advice, by saying, "Go home to your adoring husband. Spend a second honeymoon. He is waiting for you with open arms," and then thinking such pleasantries will happen.

However, I know what they don't know. I have the inside scope, and I know why I am dreading retirement.

Addendum

I WILL RETIRE WHEN I CHOOSE.

(We waited for a good get-down party)

Author: Ruth Sawh

Ruth has taught English for about 40 years. Her experience as a professor prompted this novella: *Woman Go Home.* Her writings have been divided between academic papers and creative pieces, such as short stories and poems. She authored one novel, *A Name in the Fire,* which she located in Trinidad in the Caribbean, where she was born and where she became fascinated with story tellers and the stories they concocted. She received a Ph.D. in Multilingual/Multicultural Education from Florida State University and is extremely grateful to family and friends who "lifted" her along the way. She enjoys socializing with family and friends, reading, writing, traveling, and other little pleasures of life.

Illustrator: Greg Sitkowski

I'm a self-taught cartoonist who took his idea to create the Laughing Iron universe. While creating the characters who inhabit the aforementioned universe, I was asked to teach a cartooning class. For several years I took that passion and passed it along to students both in person and virtually. Between these gaps, I wrote and illustrated four e-books and one hard cover children's book. I am an avid reader, a classic horror film buff, and a fan of retro video games. As you can tell, I am a Geek.

www.ingramcontent.com/pod-product-compliance
Lightning Source LLC
Chambersburg PA
CBHW021226130726
47988CB00002B/838